LEADER

COMMITMENT

D1617145

NOX PRESS

books for that extra kick to give you more power

www.NoxPress.com

Also by Elise Leonard:

The **JUNKYARD DAN** series: (*Nox Press*)

1. Start of a New Dan
2. Dried Blood
3. Stolen?
4. Gun in the Back
5. Plans
6. Money for Nothing
7. Stuffed Animal
8. Poison, Anyone?
9. A Picture Tells a Thousand Dollars
10. Wrapped Up
11. Finished
12. Bloody Knife
13. Taking Names and Kicking Assets
14. Mercy

THE SMITH BROTHERS (a series): (*Nox Press*)

1. All for One   5. Master Plan
2. When in Rome
3. Get a Clue
4. The Hard Way

A LEEG OF HIS OWN (a series): (*Nox Press*)

1. Croaking Bullfrogs, Hidden Robbers
2. 20,000 LEEGS Under the C
3. Failure to Lunch
4. Hamlette

The **AL'S WORLD** series: (*Simon & Schuster*)

Book 1: Monday Morning Blitz
Book 2: Killer Lunch Lady
Book 3: Scared Stiff
Book 4: Monkey Business

The **LEADER** series: (*Nox Press*)

★ Honor   ★ Integrity
★ Courage   ★ Commitment
★ Respect   ★ Loyalty
★ Service   ★ Duty

LEADER

COMMITMENT

Elise Leonard

NOX PRESS
books for that extra kick to give you more power
www.NoxPress.com

Leonard, Elise
LEADER (a series) / Commitment
ISBN: 978-1-935366-29-4

First Nox Press printing: April 2010

NOX PRESS
books for that extra kick to give you more power

**This book is dedicated to
the United States Army.**

To all of those who have served:
Thank you.

To all of those who have the wonderful traits
that are the titles of the books in this series:
Thank you.

The world becomes a better place
when people have these attributes.

So... no matter what the past brought,
or what the present holds,
or what the future brings...
be a LEADER!

~Elise

com-mit-ment –noun

1. the act of committing.
2. the state of being committed.
3. the act of committing, pledging, or engaging oneself.
4. a pledge or promise; obligation: *We have made a commitment to help you learn how to read.*
5. engagement; involvement: *Nox Press and all of the people who use and read their books have a sincere commitment to literacy.*

CHAPTER 1

The first time she saw him, she knew.

Knew he was the one.

Knew she wanted to spend the rest of her life with him.

Knew she *would* spend the rest of her life with him.

She watched him.

Watched him from across the room.

Watched every movement he made.

Every step.

Every smile.

Every turn of his head.

She just knew.

It was a feeling she had.

A deep feeling.

But one that she was sure of.

Yes. This was going to be the person she was going to spend her life with.

This was who she would tell her troubles to.

This was who she would grow old with.

This was who would guard her secrets.

This was going to be the father of her children.

She was sure.

As sure as she'd ever been about anything.

And she was sure of a lot of things.

And was usually right, too.

Which was unusual for a girl in second grade.

CHAPTER 2

"So how was your first day of school?" her mother asked.

"It was the most important day of my life," Tay said.

Her name was Taylor. But no one was named Taylor at the time.

There was no one famous with the name Taylor.

So no one had ever heard of it.

Teachers always thought it was a boy's

name.

That *really* upset her.

So she called herself Tay.

And made everyone around her call her Tay.

Her mother smiled.

"Why was it the most important day of your life? Because your teacher knew you were a girl?"

Tay's mother had called the school this time.

For the last two years, after each first day of school, her daughter had come home crying.

"The teacher thought I was a *boy*!" she'd wail.

So this year, Tay's mother had called the school.

She'd spoken with Tay's new teacher.

Telling Mrs. Clark that Taylor was a girl.

Mrs. Clark had been very nice.

She said that she would make sure Tay would not come home crying this year.

So that's what Tay's mother thought Tay was talking about.

She was shocked when she heard Tay's next words.

"No, Mom. It was the most important day of my life because I met my husband today," Tay said.

CHAPTER 3

Corina *was* shocked.

At first.

But then she laughed.

After all, Tay was only seven.

She was just a child.

This was her first day of second grade!

So Corina decided to play along.

She followed Tay to her room.

"And where did you meet this young man?"

Commitment

Tay threw her backpack on her bed.

"At school."

"Is he in your class?"

Tay nodded.

"Yes. He is in Mrs. Clark's class."

"Does he sit next to you?"

"No. He sits three rows over."

"Did you speak with him?"

"No."

"Then how do you know he will be your husband?"

"I just do."

Corina smiled.

This was just like Tay.

She was like this for seven years now.

Some would say she was stubborn.

But she wasn't stubborn.

She was just sure of herself.

She was sure of her choices.

Since the day she was born.

If Tay wanted to eat strained peas, she ate

them.

If she didn't want to eat strained carrots, she would *not* eat them.

She would just spit them out.

No matter how many times Corina tried to get her to eat strained carrots, each and every time, Tay would spit them out.

Tay couldn't read the label.

She was an infant.

But the peas always went in. And the carrots always came out.

Tay's dad, Chris, used to laugh at his wife.

He would look at her orange splotched clothes.

He would laugh at the blobs of orange goo dripping down his wife's face.

"Why do you keep trying to feed her carrots?" he'd ask.

"Because carrots are good for her."

He would laugh again.

Commitment

"But they are not good for you," he would tease.

Then he would scoop some carrots off of his wife's face.

He would eat them off his finger.

Then he would gaze at Tay.

The love he felt was clearly written on his face.

"Our baby knows what she likes."

Then he would kiss Tay's carrot-covered face.

"And she knows what she doesn't like."

Then he would turn back to his wife.

"She does *not* like strained carrots."

But Corina kept trying.

Hoping one day her baby would like carrots.

CHAPTER 4

Tay never did eat those carrots.

And the day Tay's father died in that car crash, Corina stopped trying to feed them to her.

It had nothing to do with Tay.

Or the carrots.

It had just hurt Corina too much to recall Chris.

Smiling down at his carrot-covered baby.

Loving her.

Despite the fact that she was sometimes difficult.

And it hurt Corina to recall how Chris had loved her, too.

Despite the fact that *she* was sometimes difficult.

They had had a fight that morning.

The morning that Chris had died.

It was really a stupid fight.

Not even about something important.

She had yelled at him about his work.

"You are working too many hours!" she'd screamed.

"I need the extra hours," he had replied.

"You are just trying to stay away from me and the baby!" she'd screamed.

He'd looked at his wife.

He'd shook his head.

"No, honey. I'm doing this *for* you and the baby."

She would not listen.

"You just want to stay away from us," she'd yelled. "Because *I've* gained weight and *she's* so hard to deal with!"

Corina knew she wasn't making sense.

She knew she was being ridiculous.

But she couldn't help it.

Staying at home with her baby was hard work.

And she was so tired.

Chris had tried not to smile. But he'd failed.

His warm smile spread across his face.

That smile had made Corina even more angry.

Chris hugged his wife and spoke softly.

"You are *still* the most beautiful woman I have ever seen. Even with carrots in your hair."

That made Corina *so* angry!

"Don't touch me!" she'd yelled.

She'd started to cry.

"This is hard work!" she'd yelled.

"I know it is," Chris had said. "And I thank you for taking care of our baby. You are a good mother."

"No I'm not!" she'd screamed.

"Yes you are," he'd said soothingly.

"I can't even get her to eat her carrots!"

Chris had smiled again.

"She just doesn't like carrots," he'd said.

He tried to hug his wife again.

"Don't touch me!" she'd roared. "Just go off to work! I'll do this all by myself! You don't ever have to come back here again!"

Her voice was loud and shrill.

It woke up the baby.

Tay was in her crib. She was screaming her head off.

"Now look what you've done!" Corina had said to Chris.

Those were the last words she'd said to him.

CHAPTER 5

Corina looked down at her seven year old daughter.

"This future husband of yours. Does he have a name?"

"Of course he has a name."

Corina waited.

When Tay did not say more, she spoke again.

"Would you like to *share* it?"

"One day I will, but I'm too young now,

Mom."

Corina smiled.

"I meant, would you like to *tell* me his name."

"Oh," Tay said. "Sure. It's Uquail."

"Is that his last name?"

"No. It's his first name."

"What is his last name?"

"His last name is Scott."

Tay smiled brightly.

"We all call him by his last name. Scott. It's easier."

Tay giggled.

"At first, Mrs. Clark didn't want to call him by his last name."

"What changed her mind?"

Tay grinned.

"She has to. He brought in a note from his grandfather."

Corina laughed.

"It's not funny, Mom. He doesn't have

parents. He lives with his grandpa."

That *was* sad.

"So tell me about this boy," she asked Tay.

Tay thought about that.

"He's really smart."

"How do you know?"

After all, Tay had just met him. It *was* only the first day of school.

"I can tell," Tay said.

Tay looked up at her mom.

"And he's nice too."

"Was he nice to *you*?"

"He's nice to everyone," Tay replied.

"How was he nice to you?"

"Oh," Tay said. "He didn't talk to *me* today. But I heard him talking with other kids."

Corina smiled.

She had nothing to worry about.

This was just a silly fad.

Commitment

By next week, her little Tay would be in love with someone else.

By next year, Tay will have been in love with at least ten boys.

In five years, her little Tay will have gone through fifty boys.

Maybe more.

Maybe less.

But Corina knew little girls.

After all, she'd been one once herself.

And she knew that *all* of these boys would be "the most wonderful boy in the world" in Tay's eyes.

Until they weren't.

And then her little Tay would most likely move on to the next little boy.

CHAPTER 6

But that was not what happened.

Tay and Scott became best friends in second grade.

They stayed best friends in third grade.

Same with fourth and fifth grade.

Corina thought when they got to middle school, things would change.

But she was wrong.

Tay and Scott were best friends all through middle school.

Commitment

Then high school came.

Tay and Scott worked hard during high school.

Tay had been right about Scott.

He was a *very* smart boy.

He'd worked hard in school.

His grades were good.

He would sit in Corina's kitchen and tell her he wanted to work with computers.

He was known throughout his high school.

He was the guy the kids would go to when their computers broke.

All of the teachers knew him, too.

They would ask for his help when their computers had problems.

People said Scott was a computer genius.

CHAPTER 7

Corina came home late one night.

She had been working extra hours.

Tay was still up studying.

"I thought you were ready for your test?" she asked Tay.

Tay smiled.

"I *am* ready, Mom. I just want to make sure I know it all."

Corina smiled back.

That was just like Tay. She was prepared

for the test, but wanted to study more.

Corina took off her coat.

She hung it up on the peg.

There were three pegs on the coat rack.

One for Corina's coat.

One for Tay's coat.

And one that should have been for Chris.

"Your father would have been so proud of you, Tay."

Tay looked up from her book.

She smiled at her mother.

"I made you a dinner plate," Tay said. "If you're hungry."

"Thanks," Corina said. "I'm starved."

She went to the kitchen.

She took the plastic-wrapped plate from the fridge.

"Yum," she said. "A pork chop. And macaroni and cheese."

Tay walked into the kitchen.

"Yeah," Tay said. "I also made carrots.

But I ate them all."

Corina looked at her daughter.

Tay was grinning.

"Right," Corina said. "Like I believe *that*!"

They both laughed.

Tay took the plate from her mother's hand.

She stuck it in the microwave and pressed a couple of buttons.

"Mom?" Tay said.

"Yes?"

"Sit down," Tay said.

"Don't mind if I do. My feet do ache a little today."

"You're working too hard," Tay said.

"I'm just working a few extra hours so I can get you that red prom dress."

And pay for your college, Corina thought to herself.

But then Corina's mind flew to the last

time she'd spoken with Chris. That time when she had told *him* that *he* was working too many hours.

Corina had known back then *why* he was working so hard.

But now she *felt* it.

Felt it to her core.

Felt that drive to take care of one's family.

To provide for the ones you love.

Once again, she regretted that fight she'd picked with Chris.

It was eleven years ago.

But it still hurt like it was yesterday.

Despite the fact that she'd regretted those words at least a million times.

Maybe more.

"I don't need the red dress, Mom."

"But you look so beautiful in it."

"Are you saying I don't look beautiful in the blue dress?" Tay teased.

"No."

"Then what *are* you saying?"

"I'm *saying* you look better in the red dress."

"But the red dress costs three times as much," Tay said.

The microwave's bell rang.

Tay took out the plate and placed it before her mother.

"Mmm. Smells good."

"Don't change the subject," Tay told her mom.

Tay took the applesauce from the fridge.

She got a clean spoon.

She placed both on the table.

"I don't need the red dress, Mom," Tay said sternly. "The blue dress will be great."

CHAPTER 8

Corina opened the door.

"Scott's here," she called to Tay.

She let Scott in.

"You look great," she told Scott.

"Thank you," he said shyly. "I'm not used to being in a tuxedo."

Corina smiled.

"You wear it well," she told the young man.

He blushed.

"So what are your plans?" she asked Scott.

"Well, first we'll go to the prom. Then we'll go out with our friends."

"Who will be driving?" Corina asked.

She worried about cars.

But Scott knew she had reason to, so he didn't seem to mind the question.

He didn't seem to mind *any* of her questions. He never did.

He was a good kid.

"Twelve of us chipped in for a limo," he said.

"Oh," she said. "Good planning."

Scott nodded.

"Yes, ma'am. The limo driver will take us where ever we want to go."

He took out his cell phone.

He checked the battery.

"I can have Tay call you every couple of hours, if you want. So you'll know where we are and what we're doing."

Corina was pleased.

"Yes, Scott. That would be great."

Scott nodded.

"It's no problem, ma'am. I know how you worry about her."

"Thank you," Corina said softly.

She was trying not to get teary eyed.

She was thinking of Chris, and how he would have loved to have been there.

It was a shame that he had missed this night.

Prom night.

It was a big night for a girl.

And Corina knew that every father dreams of seeing his baby girl in her prom dress.

It was with that thought that Tay came into the room.

"Oh my God," Scott said.

He stared at Tay.

"You look amazing!" he mumbled.

The boy could not take his eyes off of Tay.

She really did look quite beautiful.

Like a fairy princess.

Even Corina was shocked by how gorgeous her daughter looked.

Not that Tay wasn't a pretty girl.

She *was*.

But she looked all grown up.

She was quite stunning in her strapless red silk gown.

CHAPTER 9

Prom night did not go as planned.

"I can't believe you *did* that!" Tay screamed.

"It was my only choice," Scott said.

"No it wasn't!" Tay shouted.

"Yes it was, Tay."

"No it wasn't. You could start at the community college."

"My grandfather can't even afford *that*, Tay."

"You could have worked your way through school."

Scott tried to reason with Tay.

"That's what I'm *doing*."

"Joining the Army?! No! That's not working your way through school."

"Tay," Scott pleaded. "It was my only option."

"No it wasn't."

"My grandfather can barely afford our rent and food. How can I ask him to pay for college."

"You could have gotten loans," Tay said.

"I don't want to start our life with a lot of debt, Tay."

"Then you could have gotten a *job*!" Tay yelled. "Lots of people work their way through school."

"But this way, I get paid *and* get to learn at the same time."

Scott hugged Tay.

Commitment

"This is good for us," Scott said. "This is good for our future. You'll see."

The conversation was over. Tay didn't want to talk about it anymore.

*   *   *

The next day, Tay was restless.

"What's the matter?" Corina asked Tay.

"Nothing. I have to go somewhere," Tay said.

"Where are you going?"

"I have something I have to do," Tay said.

"I thought we were going to go to the movies."

"We will, Mom. When I get back."

Tay ran out of the house.

"Where are you going?" Corina called to her.

Tay spoke over her shoulder.

"I'll tell you when I get back."

CHAPTER 10

Tay's face was flushed.

And she was out of breath when she came home.

"So what was all that about?" Corina asked Tay.

Tay turned to her mother.

"Mom. Just hear me out."

Oh, this does not sound good, Corina thought to herself.

"And don't get mad," Tay added.

Commitment

Corina had no idea what was going on.

But she had a feeling that she *was* going to get angry.

"What did you do?!" Corina asked Tay.

"Well, you heard the fight I had with Scott last night. Right?" Tay asked her mother.

"It was hard *not* to hear it," Corina said.

"He's going into the Army," Tay said.

"Yes. I heard," Corina said slowly.

"Well, I can't live without him," Tay said.

"Tay," Corina said. "You're being a bit over-dramatic. Don't you think?"

"No," Tay said. "We have been together every day since second grade."

"But you're adults now."

Tay sighed.

"Mom. He's been in my life since I was seven. He is a part of me. Like my arm. Or my leg. Or my heart."

Tay looked at her mother.

"I can't *live* without my arm or leg or heart."

Corina looked at her child.

"Taylor, honey, you *could* live without your arm or leg."

"But I couldn't live without my heart, Mom."

Corina tried to slow this conversation down. It was flying out of control.

And to be honest, it wasn't making much sense to Corina.

Before she could solve the problem, she had to know what the problem *was*.

Tay was being a drama queen. And that wasn't helping things.

Corina needed facts.

"Just tell me what you did, Taylor."

Tay looked at the ground.

She knew how her mother would react to her news.

Not well.

CHAPTER 11

"I signed up for the Army."

"You did *WHAT*?!"

"The man said that I could be with Scott."

"What man?!" Corina roared.

"The guy who recruits."

"Oh my God! Oh my God! Oh my God!" Corina said.

"It's okay, Mom. He said Scott and I will be together."

"And you *believed* him?!" Corina shouted.

She didn't mean to shout.

She didn't *want* to shout.

She wanted to discuss this calmly.

But it really didn't matter how she handled this.

Tay had already signed up.

There was little Corina could do.

It was already done.

And Corina thought it was a mistake.

"Why would he lie?" Tay asked.

"Because he's a *recruiter*! He wants you to sign up!" Corina said.

She looked at her young daughter.

"It's his *job*!" Corina added.

Tay stormed out of the room.

She slammed her bedroom door.

Corina walked to Tay's room.

She knocked on the door.

"Tay. I'm sorry, honey," she said through

the door.

"You just don't *get* me!" Tay said. "You never have!"

Corina sighed softly.

"Please, Tay. Open the door."

The door did not open.

"I want to talk with you," Corina said softly.

"I don't want to talk to you!"

The door did not open.

Not then.

Not three hours later.

And not the next morning.

*   *   *

The last two weeks of school went quickly for Tay.

She did her final exams.

Then she and Scott got ready to go into the Army.

CHAPTER 12

It turned out that Corina was right.

Tay was *not* sent to the same place Scott was sent.

Now the young couple was not together, and they would not have a chance to *be* together.

They were *not* married, and would not see each other for at *least* six months.

Tay was crushed.

She wrote home to her mother.

Commitment

> You were right, Mom!
> They lied to me!
> What should I do now?
> Love, Tay

Corina wrote back.

> There is nothing you can
> do, my daughter.
> You signed up.
> You made a commitment.
> You cannot get out of it.
> I miss you, Tay.
> Be safe, and know I love
> you.
> Love, Mom

Meanwhile, Tay and Scott were also writing to each other.

They shared their thoughts.

They shared their love.

And they shared their concerns.

When Scott got time off, Tay did not.

When Tay got time off, Scott did not.

Time flew by, and they did not see each other for eight months.

Then, something great happened.

They both got four days off.

The *same* four days off!

Scott was stationed at Fort Hood in Texas.

Tay was stationed at Fort Drum in New York.

Scott emailed Tay.

FROM: Uquail Scott

SENT: February 10 - 3:29 PM

TO: ScottsTayTerTot

SUBJECT: Valentine's Day surprise...

Tay. I bought you a plane ticket. You are meeting me in Florida. We're going to Disney. We will have three whole days together! I have a surprise for you.

Commitment

Tay emailed back to Scott.

FROM: ScottsTayTerTot

SENT: February 10 - 5:58 PM

TO: Uquail Scott

SUBJECT: RE: Valentine's Day surprise...

I'm so excited !!!!!!!!!

I can't wait to see you !!!!

Thanks for the ticket !!!!!

What's my surprise?????????

FROM: Uquail Scott

SENT: February 10 - 8:08 PM

TO: ScottsTayTerTot

SUBJECT: RE: RE: Valentine's Day surprise...

If I told you...

it WOULDN'T BE A SURPRISE!

Tay was so excited!

She was *finally* going to see Scott!

She couldn't remember a day when she was happier.

FROM: ScottsTayTerTot

SENT: February 10 - 10:34 PM

TO: Uquail Scott

SUBJECT: RE: RE: RE: Valentine's Day surprise...

Oh come on !!!!!

Just tell me !!!!!!

PLEASE !!!!!!!!!!!!!!!!!!!

I'll be your best friend.

FROM: Uquail Scott

SENT: February 10 - 11:46 PM

TO: ScottsTayTerTot

SUBJECT: RE: RE: RE: RE: Valentine's Day surprise...

NO.

And you already ARE my best friend!

But then the day came for the trip.

Tay was packed and ready to go.

There was a huge snowstorm the night before.

So getting to Syracuse Airport was nuts.

Snow was piled five feet high.

The roads were slick and icy.

But the taxi driver was nice.

"You're going to see your boyfriend?" he asked Tay.

"Yes," she said. "I haven't seen him in eight months."

"That's a long time."

"Yes. We were together every day for eleven years before that."

"Eleven years?!" he said. "You don't look that old."

Tay laughed.

"I'm not," Tay said.

They finally got to the airport.

CHAPTER 13

"Good luck to you and your fellow," the cab driver said.

"Thank you," Tay said.

She tipped him well.

"And thank you for getting me here safe and sound," she said.

"Thank *you*," the man said. "It was my pleasure."

But just because Tay had made it to the airport, it didn't mean that her flight would go off as scheduled.

And... it didn't.

The airport could not get the runways shoveled fast enough.

Her flight was delayed.

She was so frustrated.

So close, and yet, so far.

And she knew Scott was waiting for her.

She called his cell phone.

"My flight has been delayed," she wailed into the phone.

"Okay," Scott said. "We can deal with this."

"No we can't!" Tay shrieked. "With every hour that goes by, it's one hour less we have together."

"How long is the delay?"

"First it said one hour. Then they changed it to three. Now it just says delayed... with no departure time. I'm afraid they will cancel the flight."

"Okay," Scott said. "Let me see what I can do. I'll call you back."

"What can you do?!" Tay said into the phone.

But Scott had already hung up.

About twenty minutes later, he called her back.

"I have a friend," he said. "He will take you in a bird."

"A bird?" Tay asked.

"A helicopter," Scott said. "He can only take you to Tampa, Florida."

"Tampa?!" Tay said. "Why Tampa?"

"He's in the Air Force. And he's going to MacDill. That's in Tampa," Scott said.

"I thought you were in Orlando?"

"I *am* in Orlando. But I can get to Tampa."

"So Disney World is out?" Tay asked.

"Yes, Tay. I'm sorry."

"Was that my surprise?"

Scott laughed.

"No," he said.

"Will I still get my surprise?" Tay asked Scott.

"I'm working on it, babe!" he replied.

Tay was so bummed out. This was not going as planned.

And she *really* was looking forward to this.

"Will I like my surprise?"

Scott laughed again.

"I think you will," he said.

Then he chuckled.

"At least, I *hope* you will!" he added.

CHAPTER 14

The chopper showed up a half hour later.

Tay got her luggage and walked to the chopper.

She was sliding on the ice patches.

A man got out to help her get into the helicopter.

"A bird beats a plane every time," the man said.

He pointed to the ice.

"And that's one good reason why."

Commitment

Tay smiled widely.

She was happy because she would see her Scott soon.

"So you are Scott's Tay," he said to Tay.

Tay nodded.

"Yes, that's me."

"Are you two really together since the second grade?" the man asked.

Tay smiled.

"Yes, sir," she said.

"Well, we'll see if we can't get you two back together again."

Another man laughed.

"We're not like all the king's horses and all the king's men," he said.

Tay looked at him.

"Excuse me?" she asked.

The guys laughed.

"Don't listen to him. His kid is in the school play."

"My son got the leading part!" the man

bragged.

Tay smiled.

"How nice! What play are they doing?"

"Humpty Dumpty."

"And he's Humpty Dumpty?" Tay asked the man.

"Sure is," the soldier said proudly.

Another man started to laugh.

"He's been practicing his lines like a lunatic."

"Well," Tay said. "He doesn't want to mess up his part."

"Not the *boy*!" the man said. "*This* one's been practicing his lines like a lunatic."

He hitched his thumb at the proud dad.

"Humpty Dumpty sat on a wall. Humpty Dumpty had a great fall. All the king's horses and all the king's men..."

The chopper took off.

It was rising in the air.

The noise was deafening.

CHAPTER 15

When the chopper landed in Tampa, Scott was waiting.

Tay flew from the chopper right into Scott's arms.

The men caught up soon after.

"See? We *could* get these two back together again!"

Then Tay got it.

"All the king's horses and all the king's men, couldn't put Humpty together again."

"But we *did* get you two back together again. So we're not like all the king's horses and all the king's men."

Tay was beaming.

"I'm sure your son will make a great Humpty Dumpty," she said.

Scott turned around and nodded.

"Are you ready for your surprise?" he asked Tay.

"Sure am!"

A man came over to the group.

"Can we take this somewhere off the tarmac?" the man asked.

Scott laughed.

"Yes, sir," he said. "But Tay might want to hit the ladies room first."

She did not want to leave Scott just yet.

Even if she did have to go.

"No, I'm good," Tay said.

Scott laughed.

"Your mother's right," he said. "You

really *can* be kind of stubborn."

"Why?" Tay asked. "Because I don't want to go to the ladies room?"

Scott laughed.

He looked at the man.

"Can you help me out here, sir?"

This whole trip was not going as planned.

All Tay wanted was to be alone with Scott.

It was okay that they didn't go to Disney World.

But she *would* have liked a little time alone with Scott!

"If you want me to go to the ladies room so badly, I'll go to the ladies room!" she said.

Maybe the crowd would break up while she was in there.

And maybe she and Scott could be alone when she got out.

That would be nice.

So Tay bustled off to the ladies room.

The sooner she went in there, the sooner she would come out.

And the sooner Scott and Tay could start their vacation together.

But that's not what happened.

CHAPTER 16

Tay was shocked when she went in the ladies room.

Her mom was standing there.

Holding a wedding dress.

"So?" Corina asked Tay. "What do you think?"

Before Tay could answer, she turned on her heel.

She ran out of the bathroom.

Scott was waiting for her.

He was on one knee.

"Tay, would you do me the honor of being my wife?" Scott asked.

Tay's smile was huge.

It looked like her face would crack in two.

"Is this my surprise?" Tay asked.

She looked around.

Her mom had also come out of the bathroom.

She was wearing a beautiful dress.

Like she was dressed up for a wedding.

Scott's grandfather was also there.

He was wearing an old, worn suit.

He looked great.

Older. Smaller.

More hunched over.

But great.

"I *love* my surprise," Tay gushed.

She was beaming with happiness.

"And I love *you*," she told Scott.

Commitment

Scott stayed kneeling.

"I've loved you since the first time I saw you," Tay said.

She looked down at Scott.

"And I knew you would be my husband."

Scott looked up at Tay.

"Tay?" he asked.

"Yes?" she whispered.

"Would you *please* answer the question I asked you?"

Tay laughed.

"I thought I *had* answered it."

"Nope. You really didn't," Scott said.

Tay laughed freely.

"Yes, Uquail Scott. I will most *certainly* marry you."

Scott grinned.

"Thanks."

The man from before came over to the young couple.

"Once you get dressed, Tay, I will perform the ceremony," he said.

Tay didn't need anything more to be said.

She ran—full blast—back into the ladies room to put on her gown.

"It fits *perfectly*!" Tay said.

"I had them use your prom gown for the measurements," Corina said.

"It's so gorgeous!" Tay said.

"The dress is pretty," Corina said. "The woman *in* the dress is gorgeous."

CHAPTER 17

Since they couldn't honeymoon at Disney World, they settled for a day at Busch Gardens and a stay at the Tampa Hilton.

Tay thought it was the perfect wedding.

So did Scott.

But all too soon, their time together was up.

They both had to return back to work.

But at least they were now married.

Tay had that to hold on to.

FROM: Uquail Scott

SENT: February 28 - 6:42 AM

TO: ScottsTayTerTot

SUBJECT: How's my TayTerTot?

How's my TayTerTot?

Miss me?

I sure do miss you!

Tay emailed back to Scott.

FROM: ScottsTayTerTot

SENT: February 28 - 10:22 AM

TO: Uquail Scott

SUBJECT: RE: How's my TayTerTot?

    That's MRS. ScottsTayTerTot to you !!!!!!!!!

    And yes, I miss you !!!!!!!!!!!!!!!!!!

    I miss you tons !!!!!!!!!!!!!!

Their emails went pretty much like that for the next two months.

Until...

Commitment

FROM: ScottsTayTerTot

SENT: April 26 - 7:38 PM

TO: Uquail Scott

SUBJECT: I need to tell you something !!!!!

I tried to call you, but you didn't pick up.

I HAVE to tell you ASAP !!!!!!!

I went to the urgent care clinic today. Was feeling

sick. Like I had the flu.

FROM: Uquail Scott

SENT: April 26 - 8:53 PM

TO: ScottsTayTerTot

SUBJECT: RE: I need to tell you something !!!!!

Are you okay? I'm worried about you.

Do you have the flu?

FROM: ScottsTayTerTot

SENT: April 26 - 9:17 PM

TO: Uquail Scott

SUBJECT: RE: RE: I need to tell you something !!!!!

ScottsTayTerTot is having a REAL tot !!!!!!!!

CHAPTER 18

"This is so cool! I'm going to be a *dad*!" Scott said. "How did this happen?!"

"Well, remember that night, in Tampa, at the Hilton?"

Scott laughed.

"I know *how* it happened," he said.

"So what's your question?" Tay asked.

Scott laughed again.

"I guess I don't have a question," he said. "But Tay?"

Commitment

"Yeah?"

"Don't freak out when I say this. But..."

He paused to gather his thoughts.

"I'm going to be a father now, and I've made a commitment to you and... the baby."

"So?" Tay asked.

"And I know you were mad when I signed up. But I've learned a lot. And I'm doing really well in the Army."

He waited for her to say something.

She didn't.

"And I make good money," he added.

"So?"

"So, would you be mad if I make a career of the Army?"

"Is this what you want to do?" Tay asked.

"Yes."

"Would you do this if we *weren't* going to have a baby?"

"Yes."

"Then of course I don't mind."

Seven months later, Tay was home for maternity leave.

She had four months off.

She would have the baby, then stay at home for four months.

Then she would return to Fort Drum.

Corina would take care of the baby until Tay's commitment to the Army was done.

Then Tay would go home and get their child.

Then Tay and the baby would join Scott.

They would finally be a real family.

A normal family.

A *regular* family.

Tay couldn't wait!

She had just returned home.

The baby was due the next week.

Tay was sitting on the couch with her feet up.

She was reading a book about baby care.

Commitment

Corina rushed though the door.

"Have you heard from Scott?" she asked.

"No," Tay said. "He's not coming home until after the baby is born. You know that, Mom. Are you losing it?"

Corina did not smile.

"Have you heard the news today?" she asked Tay.

"No, why?"

Corina flew to the TV.

She clicked it on.

Scenes of people running around flashed across the screen.

Scenes of bodies lying on the ground flashed across the screen.

Police officers were running all over the place.

Men and women in uniform were running all over the place.

"What's going on?" Tay asked.

Corina didn't answer.

The words FORT HOOD flashed across the screen.

"Oh my God!" Tay screamed.

She reached for her phone.

She dialed Scott's work number.

No one answered.

She tried his cell phone.

It rang and rang.

Then it went to voice mail.

"Scott, it's Tay, please call home. I'm worried about you. Are you okay? What's going on up there? Please call home as soon as you can."

Tay's phone rang three hours later.

"Mrs. Scott?" the male voice said.

"Yes," she whispered.

"This is the chaplain from Fort Hood," he said.

A scream escaped from Tay's mouth.

Her heart started beating wildly.

And then she went into labor.

CHAPTER 19

Three months later, Tay spoke with her mother.

"Mom?"

"Yes, Tay?"

"I'm not going to be able to leave him here."

Corina smiled sadly. "I had a feeling that would happen."

She gazed at her beautiful grandson.

"You named him well," Corina said.

Tay laughed.

"Uquail Scott, Jr. is the spitting image of his father," Corina noted.

"Mom?" Tay asked softly.

Corina tore her eyes from her grandson.

"Is there any way you will go back to Fort Drum with me?" Tay asked.

Corina brightened.

"Do you want me there?" Corina asked.

"Yes," Tay said.

"But then what will we do when your commitment to the Army is over?" Corina asked.

Tay looked at her mother.

"About that," Tay said.

She looked shyly at Corina.

"Scott was serious about his commitment to the Army. I thought I'd re-enlist in honor of his commitment."

"I think Scott would have liked that," Corina said.

We hope you liked this book in the

LEADER

series.

We hope you will read
all the books in the series:

HONOR
COURAGE
RESPECT
SERVICE
INTEGRITY
COMMITMENT
LOYALTY
DUTY

Want comedies?

Try reading...

THE SMITH BROTHERS

We also have...

the very funny

A LEEG
OF HIS OWN

series.

Everyone has it
within them
to be a

LEADER

Do you?

And if you haven't
read them yet,
you might want to
check out...

Junkyard Dan

(A series of comedic crime dramas.)

NOX PRESS

books for that extra kick to give you more power

www.NoxPress.com

Want to read more
NOX PRESS
books?

Go online to
www.NoxPress.com
to see what's being released!

Books can easily be purchased online
or you can contact **Nox Press**
via the Website for quantity discounts.

Are you a fan?
Do you want us to put *your* comments
up on our Website?
If so, please e-mail them to:
NoxPress@gmail.com

NOX PRESS
books for that extra kick to give you more power
www.NoxPress.com